THE
BUCKLED BAG

BY

MARY

ROBERTS

RINEHART

BLACKBIRD BOOKS
NEW YORK • LOS ANGELES

A Blackbird Classic, May 2024

Manufactured in the United States of America.

The events and characters depicted in this book are
fictional.

Cataloging-in-Publication Data

Rinehart, Mary Roberts.
The buckled bag / Mary Roberts Rinehart.
p. cm.
1. Detective and mystery stories.
2. Nurses—Fiction.
3. Women detectives—Fiction. I. Title.
PS3535.I73 B83 2024 813′.54—dc23 2024931829

Blackbird Books
www.bbirdbooks.com
email us at editor@bbirdbooks.com

ISBN 978-1-61053-047-7

First Blackbird Edition

10 9 8 7 6 5 4 3 2 1

THE
BUCKLED BAG

I

I have broken down in health lately—nothing serious, but a nurse lasts only so long, and during the last five years, I have been under a double strain. Caring for the sick has been only a part of it. The other?

Well, put it like this: The world's pretty crowded after all. We are always touching elbows, and there is never a deviation from the usual, the normal, that is not felt all the way down the line. Stand a row of dominoes on edge, and knock down the end one. Do you see? And generally, somebody goes down for fair. We do not know much about it among the poor; they have to manage the best way they can, and maybe they are blunted—some of them. They have not the time for mental agony. And the thing works both ways. Their lapses are generally obvious—cause and result; motive and crime.

In the lower walks of life, people are more elemental. But get up higher. Crime exists there, but, instead of a passion, it is a craft. In its detection, it is brain against brain, not intellect against brute force or instinct. If anything gives, it is the body.

Illness follows crime—it does not always follow the criminal, but somebody goes down for fair. There is a breach in the wall. The doctor and the clergyman come in then. One way and another they get the story. There is nothing hidden from them. They get it, but they do not want it. They cannot use it. The clergyman's vows and the medical man's legal status forbid their using their knowledge, but, where a few years ago, there were only two, now each crisis, mental or physical, finds three—the trained nurse.

Do you see what I mean? The thing is thrust at her. She does not want the story either. Her business is bodies, doctors' orders, nourishments, but unless she's a fool, she ends by holding the family secret in the hollow of her hand. It worries her. She needs her hands. She gets rid of it as soon as she can and forgets it. She is safe; the secret is safe. Without the clergyman's vows or the doctor's legal status, she is as silent as either.

That is the ethical side. That is what the nurse does. There is another side, which is mine. The criminal uses every means against society. Why not society against the criminal? And this is my defense. Every trained nurse plays a game, a sort of sporting proposition—her wits against wretchedness. I play a double game—the fight against misery and the fight against crime—like a man running two chessboards at once.

I hated it in the beginning. It has me by the throat now. It is the criminal I find absorbing. And I have learned some things—not new, of course: that to be honest because one is untempted is to be strong with the strength of a child; that the great virtues often link arms with the great vices; that the big criminal thinks big thoughts.

I have had my chance to learn, and I know. A nurse gets under the very skin of the soul. She finds a mind surrendered, all the crooked little motives that have fired the guns of life revealed in their pitifulness. Even now, sometimes, it hurts me to look back.

It is five years since George L. Patton was shot in the leg during a raid on the Hengst Place, in

Cherry Run. He is at the head of one of the big private agencies now, but he was a county detective then, and Hengst shot him from a cupboard. Well, that does not matter particularly, except that Mr. Patton was brought to the hospital that night and I was given the case.

He took it very calmly, said he guessed he would rest awhile, now that he had the chance, and slept eighteen hours without moving. I made caps, I remember, and tried to plan what I would do when I left the house. My time was about up, and I dreaded private duty. I had been accustomed to the excitement of a hospital, and there was something horrible to me in the idea of spending the rest of my life in darkened rooms, with the doctor's daily visit for excitement and a walk round the block for recreation.

I gave Mr. Patton his dinner that night and we had our first clash. He looked at the soup and toast, and demanded steak and onions.

"I'm sorry," I said. "You're to have light diet for a day or two. We don't want any fever from that leg."

"Leg! What has my leg to do with my stomach? I want a medium steak. I'll do without the onions if I have to."

"Doctor's orders," I said firmly. "You may have an egg custard if you want it, or some cornstarch."

We had a downright argument, and he took the soup. When he had finished, he looked up at me and smiled.

"I don't like you," he said, "but darned if I don't respect you, young woman. Absolute obedience to orders is about the hardest thing in the world to get. And now send for that fool intern, and we'll have a steak for breakfast."

Well, he did, and pretty soon he was getting about everything the hospital could give him. He was a politician, of course, and we depended on our state appropriation for support, but he got nothing from me without an order. He always said he did not like me, but I think he did after a while. I could beat him at chess, for one thing.

"You have a good head, Miss Adams," he said to me one day when he was almost well. "Are you going to spend the rest of your life changing pillowcases and shaking down thermometers?"

"I've thought of institutional work; I dare say I'd be changing nurses and shaking down interns," I said with some bitterness.

"How old are you?—not, of course, for publication."

"Twenty-nine."

"Any family?"

"The nearest relatives I have are two old aunts, in the country."

He was silent for a minute or two. Then: "I've been thinking of something; I may take it up with you later. There's only one objection—you're rather too good-looking."

"I'm not really good-looking at all," I admitted frankly. "I have too high a forehead. It's the cap."

"Like 'em high!" said Mr. Patton.

I made an eggnog and brought it in to him. He was sitting propped in a chair, and when I gave him the glass, he smiled up at me. He had never attempted any sentimentalities with me, which is more than can be said of the usual convalescent male over forty.

"It isn't all the cap," he said.

That afternoon, he tried to learn from me something about the other patients on the floor, but, of course, I would tell him nothing. He seemed rather irritated and tried to bully me, but I was firm.

"Don't be childish, Mr. Patton!" I said at last. "We don't tell about other patients. If you want to find out, get one of your men in here." To my surprise he laughed.

"Good girl!" he said. "You've stood a cracking test and come through A1. You've got silence and obedience to orders, and you have a brain. I've mentioned the forehead. Now I'm going to make my proposition. Has it ever occurred to you that every crisis, practically, among the better classes, finds a trained nurse on hand?"

"Cause or result?"

"Result, of course. Upset the ordinary routine of a family, have a robbery, an elopement, or a murder, and somebody goes to bed, with a trained nurse in attendance. Fact, isn't it?" I admitted it. "It's a fault of the tension people live under," he went on. "Any extra strain and something snaps. And who is it who is in the very bosom of the family? You know and I know. The nurse gets it all—the intimate details that the police miss; the family disputes, the inner motives; the—you go to your room and think it over. And when you decide, I have a case for you."

I tried to object, but he cut me short; so I put the thermometer in his mouth and managed to tell him how I felt.

"It just doesn't seem honest," I finished. "I'm in a position of confidence and I violate it. That's the truth. A nurse is supposed to work for good; if she has any place, it's an uplift—if you can see what I mean. And to go into a house and pry out its secrets—"

He jerked the thermometer out wrathfully.

"Uplift!" he said. "Isn't it uplifting to place a criminal where he won't injure society? If you can't see it that way, we don't want you. Now go away and think about it."

I went up to my room and stood in front of the mirror, which is where I do most of my thinking. I talk things over with myself, I suppose. And I saw the lines beside my ears that said, "Twenty-nine, almost thirty!"—and the rows of caps ready for private duty, with only the doctor's visits for excitement and a walk round the block for recreation. And I thought of institutional work, with its daily round of small worries, its monotonous years, with my soul gradually shrinking and shaping itself to fit a set of rules. And over against it all I put Mr. Patton's offer.

I recall it all—the color that came to my face at the chance to use my head instead of only a trained obedience to orders; the prospect of adventure; the chance to pit my wits against other wits and perhaps win out. I put on one of the new caps and went down to Mr. Patton's room.

"I'll do it!" I said calmly.

My time was up two days later. Mr. Patton was practically well and gave me my instructions while I helped him pack his bag.

"Do the things the other nurses do," he advised. "Go to the Nurses' Home, but don't register for cases right away. Make an excuse that you're tired and need a few days' rest. When I telephone you, I shall call myself Doctor Patton—not that I pretend to do any medical work, but for extra caution."

"You said you had a case for me."

"I had, but it isn't big enough. I want you for something worthwhile, and it will be along soon. It's about due."

"And—just one thing, Mr. Patton: I will take my first case on trial. If I find that I am doing harm and not good by revealing the secrets of a family, I shall give it up. A doctor would be answerable to the law for doing the things I am about to do."

"You have no legal status."

"I have a moral status," I replied grimly, and he found no answer to that.

Before he left, however, he said something that rather cheered me.

"You will never be required to tell anything you learn, except what is directly pertinent to the matter in hand," he said. "I would not give such latitude to any other woman I know—but you have brains and you will know what we want."

"I cannot work in the dark—I must know what you are after."

"We will lay all our cards on your table face up. I wouldn't insult you by asking you to play blindfolded. And remember this, Miss Adams—it's as high a duty to explore and heal the moral sores of a community as it is to probe and dress, for instance, the wound of a man who has been shot in the leg."

Two days later I left the hospital and took a room at the Nurses' Home he had recommended. He would arrange with the secretary, he said, that I should be called for any case on which he wished me placed.

I put in a bad week. One of the staff of the hospital located me and called me to a case. I got out of it by saying I needed a few days' rest, and he rang off irritably. Then, on the third day, I had my handbag cut off my arm in a department store, and went home depressed and ill-humored.

"You're a fine detective!" I said to myself in the mirror, "You're not so clever as Mr. Patton thinks, and if you're honest, you'll go and tell him so."

I think I should have done so—I was so abashed—but our arrangement was that I should not try to see him under any circumstances. There was to be no suspicion of me in any way. He would see me when necessary. I still had the strap of my bag, which had been left hanging to my arm, and, as a constant reminder, I fastened it to the frame of my mirror. Even now, when the department gives me its best cases, and when I have been successful enough to justify a little pride, I look at that bit of leather and become meek and normal again.

II

In spite of Mr. Patton's promise, I went on my first case for him without any preparation. Miss Shinn, the secretary, asked me if I would take a case that evening.

"For whom?"

She was turning over the pages of her ledger in the parlor-office of the Home, and she did not look up.

"A Doctor Patton telephoned," she said. "I believe he had spoken to you of the case."

My throat tightened, but, after all, this was what I had been waiting for.

"Do you know what sort of case it is?" I asked. "I'm not doing obstetrics, you know."

"It is not an obstetric case. You are to take a taxicab at eight o'clock tonight."

Miss Shinn was a heavy, rather bilious brunette, who rarely smiled, but I caught an amused twinkle as she glanced up. Quite suddenly, I liked her. Clearly she knew what I was about to do, and she did not disapprove. And yet she was a very ethical person. I gathered that she would be very hard on a nurse who wore frivolous uniforms, or gossiped about her patients, or went to the theater with a doctor, or cut rates. And yet she was indulgent to me—she was more than indulgent. I was certain, somehow, from the very quiver of her wide back as she marked me "Engaged" on her register, that she was wildly interested and curious. It gave me confidence.

At eight o'clock that evening, I went downstairs with my suitcase and ordered a taxicab. No word had come from Mr. Patton and I had nothing but a name and address to go by. The name—we will call it G. W. March. It was not, of course. You would know the name at once if I told it. The address was a street fronting one of the parks—a good neighborhood, I knew—old families, substantial properties, traditions, all that sort of thing. Certainly not a place to look for crime.

As I waited for the cab, I searched the newspapers for something to throw light on my new enterprise. There was nothing at all except a notice that Mr. and Mrs. George W. March had returned from their summer home on the Maine coast a few days before and had opened their city home.

It looked like a robbery. I was vaguely disappointed. I had it all worked out in five minutes—Mrs. March in bed, collapsed; missing pictures or jewels; house full of trusted servants; and myself trying to solve the mystery between an alcohol rub and a dose of bromide. I hated to go on with it, but I was ashamed not to. I said to myself savagely that I was not a quitter and got into the taxicab.

The March case was not a robbery, however. It was, strictly speaking, not a criminal case at all. It concerned the disappearance of a girl, and in some ways, it was a remarkable mystery—particularly baffling because for so long, it seemed to be a result without a cause. How we found the cause at last; how we located the family in Brickyard Road and solved the puzzle of the buckled bag; how we learned the identity of the little old woman with the jet bonnet, and her connection with the garden door—all this makes up the record of my first case.

The buckled bag is lying on my desk now. It is a shabby, quaint old bag, about eight inches long, round-bellied, brown with wear. It still contains what was in it when Mr. Patton found it: a cotton handkerchief, marked with a J; two keys—one a house door key, the other a flat one; a scrawled note in a soiled lavender envelope; a newspaper clipping of a sale of blankets.

It is one of my most painful memories that for a month, I examined that newspaper cutting frequently and that I failed entirely to grasp the significance of the reverse side. We all have a mental blind spot. That was mine.

Clare March was missing. That was my case: to find her, or to help to find her, was my task at first. Later it grew more complicated. I had not thought Mr. Patton would violate our agreement about working in the dark, and my confidence was justified. At the first corner, he hailed the machine and got in.

"Fine work!" he said. "You're a dependable person, Miss Adams."

"I'm rather a scared person."

"Nonsense! And don't take yourself or this affair too seriously. Do your durnedest—'Angels could do no more.'"

"Is it something stolen?"

"A small matter of a daughter. It's a queer thing, Miss Adams. I'll tell you about it." He asked the driver to go slowly. "Time us to get there at eight thirty," he said. "Now, Miss Adams, here are the facts: You are going to the home of George March, the banker. You probably know the name. Mrs. March is your patient. She's not ill; she's hysterical and frightened—that's all. It's not a hard case."

"It's the hardest sort of a case."

"Well, you like work," he replied cheerfully. "The family has been away for four months. Until a month ago, Clare, the daughter, was with them. One month ago, on the third of September, Clare, who is an only child, twenty years old, left the country place in Maine for home. She traveled alone, leaving her maid in the country. The city house had not been closed; a housekeeper and two maids were there through the summer. She was expected at the house for breakfast on the morning of the fourth. She did not arrive—or, rather, she did not go home. She reached the city safely. We have traced her into the railroad station and out again—and that has been about all. She's not been seen since."

"Perhaps she has eloped."

"Possibly, but the man she is engaged to is in the city, almost frantic. Besides, there is more than I have told you. We know that she took a taxicab at the station; that before she got in, she met and accepted a small parcel from a blond young man, rather shabbily dressed; and that they seemed to be having an argument, though a quiet one. We have found the taxicab she took, and a shop where she bought a couple of books—a Browning and a recent novel. From the bookshop, she went to a department store. There she dismissed the taxicab. We have traced her in the store to a department where she bought a pair of blankets. They made a large parcel, but she took it with her. From that time, we have lost her absolutely."

"The third of September, and this is the fifth of October—almost five weeks!"

"Exactly," he said dryly. "That's why I've sent for you. We have tried all the usual things—we've combed the city fine—and we are just where we started. If we could make a noise about it, we should have some chance. Set the general public looking— that's the way to get information. You get a million clues worth nothing, and out of the lot, one that helps. But you know these people. They won't listen to any publicity. They have only one argument—if she is dead, publicity won't help her, and if she is alive, it will hurt her."

I was conscious of a vague disappointment. In the last half hour I had keyed myself to the highest pitch. I was seeing red, really—nothing but the bloodiest sort of crime would have come up to my expectation. Certainly nothing less than a murder had been in my thoughts.

"I don't see how I can help," I said, a bit resentfully. "You've had five weeks and got nowhere," I continued, "and if you are going to ask me to put myself in her place, and try to imagine what could have happened, and to follow her mental processes, I can't do it. I can't imagine myself idle and rich and twenty. I can't imagine taking a taxicab when a streetcar would do, or having a lady's maid—"

Mr. Patton laid a hand on my arm.

"Did you ever hear Lincoln's story of the little Mississippi steamboat with a whistle so large that every time they blew it the boat stopped? No? Well, no matter. I don't want you to put yourself in her place; I want a little inside help—that's all. There's a curious story behind this case, Miss Adams. We've only scratched the top. Get in there and get their confidence. They won't talk to me—too much family pride. Get the mother to talk. That's part of her trouble—family pride and bottling up her emotions. I can't get close to any of them. After five weeks,

Mrs. March still calls me Mr. Peyton." He smiled ruefully.

"She bought blankets! That's curious, isn't it?"

"It's almost ridiculous under the circumstances. You may not be able to imagine yourself twenty, and so on, but you can certainly get your wits to work on those blankets. If she had bought a revolver now—but blankets!"

"She was engaged, you say? Were there any other men who—who liked her?"

"Half a dozen, I believe—all accounted for."

"Any neurasthenic tendency?"

"In the half dozen? I dare say yes, when she announced her engagement; in the girl—I think not. She was temperamental rather. The picture I get of her is of an attractive and indulged young woman, engaged to a man she seems to have cared about. And yet, with all the gods smiling, she disappears."

I sat thoughtful. The cab was moving along beside the park now. We were almost there.

"She may be dead," I said at last.

"She may, indeed."

He rapped on the window, and when the driver stopped, he got out with a quick handshake.

"Now go to it!" he said. "Go out for a breath of air between seven and eight each evening, and—keep your eyes open. I have a hunch that you'll get this thing—beginner's luck."

The March house was an old-fashioned, rather stately residence. Instead of going upstairs to the drawing room, there was a reception room opening into the lower hall. Behind that was a music room and, still farther back, a library.

At the very rear of the lower floor was a dining room, quite the largest room in the house, extending as it did the entire width of the building. In it was a large bay window looking out onto a city garden, and in the bay, shut off by tall plants, was a small table, where the family breakfasted and even, when alone, sometimes dined.

A long flight of stairs, uncarpeted, led to the second floor. On that first evening, I got merely the vaguest outlines of the house, of course. It was silent, immaculate, rather heavy. I had a glimpse of two men in the library talking—one middle-aged, rather stout; the other much younger. Over everything, hung the hush of suspense—that hush which accompanies birth and death and great trouble.

A parlor maid admitted me and led me upstairs to my room.

"Mr. March would like to see you in the library when you have taken off your things," she said.

I changed quickly into my uniform—all white, of course, with rubber-soled white shoes. With the familiar garb, I was myself again; I could face anything, do anything. Clothes are queer things.

Mr. March turned when he heard me at the door and rose.

"I am Miss Adams, the nurse," I said. "Do you wish to see me?"

"Will you come in, Miss Adams? This is Mr. Plummer. Have you seen Mrs. March?"

"No; I thought it best to see you first."

"I am glad of that. Perhaps I ought to tell you— we are in great trouble, Miss Adams. Our—our only daughter has gone away, disappeared. It is over a month since—" He stopped.

"That is very terrible," I said. I liked his face.

"We wish absolute secrecy—of course, I need hardly say that, but you understand Mrs. March is highly nervous. I—I hope you can quiet her. What we want you to do is to be as cheerful and optimistic as possible. You know what I mean. She will talk to you about Clare—about Miss March. Reassure her if you can. Be certain that Miss March will be found soon."

"I will do what I can. Has the doctor left any orders?"

"Very few. She is to be soothed. There's a bromide, I believe. Her maid has the instructions."

There was nothing for me in that glimpse of the two men most nearly concerned—two gentlemen unaffectedly distressed and under great strain in a quiet, well-ordered house. It looked like poor material, from Mr. Patton's point of view. Mr. March followed me into the hall. "If you need anything, let me know, Miss Adams. Or will you speak to the servants?"

"I can tell better later on. If I am going to be up tonight—and I think I'd better be, this first night anyhow—I should like a lunch; something cold on a tray."

"Do you wish it upstairs?"

I hesitated. There was a picture in a silver frame on the library table—I thought it probably one of the missing girl. I wanted to see it. "It will be a change to come down."

"Very well," he said. "There will be a supper left in the dining room. There is a small table there in the bay window. It will be more comfortable—not quite so lonely."

"Thank you," I replied and started upstairs. Opposite the library door, I glanced in. I had been right about the picture. Mr. Plummer had picked it up and was looking at it. I felt certain that he was the fiancé—a manly-looking fellow; not very tall, but solid and dependable-looking, with a good head and earnest eyes.

My patient was in bed—a pretty little woman in a frilly bed jacket, with a pink light beside her. She held out a nervous hand.

"How big and strong and competent you look!" she said, and quite unexpectedly fell to crying. I had a difficult evening. She was entirely unstrung—must have me sit down by the bed at once and listen to the trouble, as she called it—and as it was, indeed.

"She wouldn't go away and leave me like this!" she said more than once. "If you only knew her, Miss Adams—so full of character, so determined, so gifted! And beautiful—haven't you seen her picture in the newspapers?"

I evaded that—I never read society news.

"And happy, too?" I said. "She must have been very happy."

I saw a change in Mrs. March's rather childish face.

"We thought she was, of course, but lately—I've remembered so many things while I've been lying here. She was very strange all summer—moody sometimes, and again so gay that she frightened me."

"Perhaps she was gay when Mr. Plummer was there and moody when he was away."

"But he wasn't there at all. That's another thing, Miss Adams. She would not let me ask Walter up. She—she really kept him away all summer. I don't believe Mr. March told the detective that—he forgot so many things."

She wanted me to telephone this piece of information to the police at once, but I persuaded her to wait. I gave her an alcohol rub and a cup of hot milk, and, finding them without effect, I took a massage gun I found on her dressing table and ran it up and down her spine. She finally relaxed with the treatment and even asked me to use it on her face.

"I'm an old woman with all the worry," she said apologetically. "It will tone up the facial muscles, won't it? And would you mind putting some cold cream on first?"

I did not mind, and after a time she fell asleep. I was glad of a respite. In my two hours over the bed, I had accumulated many ill-assorted bits of information. I wanted time to catalogue them in my mind. I have the notes I made that night on one of my records:

C. has been missing since September third; today is October fifth—a total of thirty-two days.

Was moody all summer—would not see Mr. Plummer but wrote him daily.

She had been engaged once before, to a Wilson Page, but broke engagement. Cause of trouble not known. C. suffered much at the time. Note—Have Mr. P. look up Wilson Page.

C. usually undemonstrative, but rather affected when she said goodbye to her mother. Was she planning something, unknown to them?

But if she was planning an elopement, why did she make careful appointments with her dressmakers and milliners? Is she more crafty than they think, or was her decision made unexpectedly?

She forgot her jewel case, which she always carried with her. An inventory reveals only a part of her jewelry. She wore, when she left, only the sapphire ring Mr. Plummer gave her. She had less than a hundred dollars in cash.

"Wilson Page is dark. The man who met her in the station was thin and fair.

Her picture is on her mother's dressing table—an attractive face: dark-eyed, full of character, but rather wistful. A thoughtful face. Is she living or dead? Did she go voluntarily or was she lured away? If she went voluntarily—why?

I looked round the handsome room where my patient slept calmly, her petulant features relaxed and peaceful. I glanced across the hall to Miss Clare's room, where a light burned every evening; where an ivory dressing set, with carved monogram, was spread on the toilet table; where every luxury a young woman could demand had been gathered together for her use. And I recalled the look in the face of the man downstairs as he gazed at her picture— the tragedy in the eyes of her father. How had she gone, and why? How and why?

III

My first night at the March house was marked by a disagreeable and rather mystifying occurrence. I had got my patient quiet and asleep and had had a telephone talk with the doctor by eleven.

"There is very little to do," the doctor said. "I'll come in in the morning. Just keep her comfortable and cheerful. She needs someone to talk to. Let her talk all she wants."

I darkened the room where she lay and placed a screen in the hall outside the door, with a comfortable chair beside it and a shaded lamp. I had made up my mind to sit up for that one night at least. I had had nervous cases before, and I knew that sometime between then and morning, she would waken, and that the sight of someone alert and watchful would be a comfort.

At midnight, I took off my cap, eased my hair, and loosened my uniform collar. With the neck of my dress turned in, I was fairly comfortable. But I was hungry. I had eaten almost no dinner, but it was too early for my night supper. So I got a book from the library and read.

At two o'clock, Mrs. March was still sleeping quietly, and I decided to finally get my supper. I slipped down the stairs as noiselessly as possible. An English hall lamp was turned on in the lower hall near the music room door, and far back in the dining room, a candle light in a wall bracket showed me where to go.

My progress in my rubber-soled shoes was practically noiseless. I made my way along the hall back to the dining room. The room was very large, as I have said before, paneled in oak, with a heavy fireplace and a tapestry in an overmantel above. At one corner, beside the deep bay window, were French doors, hung with casement cloths, evidently leading out into the garden.

I was deliberate in all my movements, I remember. I went to the fireplace and stood looking up at the overmantel; I found the switch that would throw the light over my small table and thus give me a more cheerful place to eat. The bay, walled off by palms and flowering oleanders in tubs, was dark and rather uninviting at that hour. I made no particular attempt to be silent, but I dare say it is a result of my training that I make no unnecessary noise.

One of the older nurses once said to me, "When you go out on private duty, you'll have to fuss about your night supper generally. An orange and a glass of milk is about what most cooks set out. Keep them up to the mark. Insist on cold meat or sandwiches, and if there's an alcohol coffeepot, have them leave it ready. Coffee is your best friend at three in the morning, and your next best is a shawl to lay over your knees."

I was thinking of that and rather smiling when I entered the recess and sat down at the small table. I was absolutely calm and beginning to be mightily interested in my case. The tray was ready, and there was a small alcohol coffeepot with a box of matches beside it.

I lit the lamp and inspected the tray. The cook seemed to have been trained by some predecessor. There was chicken, a bit of salad, brown bread, and fruit. I ate slowly while my coffee cooked—ate with an ear toward the staircase for a sound from my patient above, and with an occasional eye toward the garden below. A late moon showed a brick terrace under the windows, and three steps lower was a formal design of flower bed and path, with a small cement circle, evidently a pool in summer. Somehow, the garden looked uncanny—bushes became figures, moving about, waving arms in the breeze. I was a distinct object from outside as I sat in my nook. Having eaten and waiting only for the coffee, I stood up and extinguished the light over my head.

It was then, still standing, that I saw the hand. It was coming down the staircase rail, moving slowly and grasping tight. It was near the music room when I saw it first, and therefore going away from me, but descending. There was something terribly stealthy about it. It must have been that quality in it which made me shrink back behind an oleander. Surely there was nothing unusual in people being about in a house where there was both illness and trouble, and yet . . .

At the foot of the stairs, the hand, still on the rail, hesitated, disappeared. A moment later, there rounded the newel post a little old woman dressed in black. She limped slightly, but for all that, she came swiftly. Every detail is stamped on my mind. I can see her now, bent forward, something that was probably jet on her old-fashioned bonnet catching the faint light as she came. She had on a quaint loose black wrap—a dolman, I think they used to call them—and hanging to her arm, a shabby leather handbag.

Stealthy as her movements were, they were extremely natural. Just inside the door, she stopped, took off her spectacles, and put them in a case, which she put in her bag, and then extracted from it another pair, which she put on. The bag was a quaint one, fastened with two straps and steel buckles. The buckles were troublesome, and she was in a hurry. More than once, she turned and looked back.

I waited for her to see me. It was an old servant, of course, come to tell me I was wanted upstairs. I was so sure of it that I bent down and put out my alcohol lamp. When I straightened up, she had passed the bay and was at the French door leading to the garden. She opened the door, went out, closed it noiselessly behind her, and was gone. I tried to see her in the garden, but if she went that way, she was lost in the shadows.

Even then, I was rather amused than puzzled. I went over to the door and tried it. There was a lock on it. Unless she had a key, she had locked herself out.

I drank my coffee and went upstairs. My patient was still asleep. From Mr. March's room came heavy, deep breathing, telling that he was forgetting his anxieties, for a time at least. But my book—the book I had left on my chair in the hall—was gone!

It seemed rather absurd. I thought I might have taken it with me, and I searched the dining room, without result. It was not to be found. I thought of the little old housekeeper, or whatever she was—but that was ridiculous. Besides, she had carried no book. She had a black leather handbag over her arm. She might, of course, have put the book—what idiocy was I thinking! The book must be somewhere about. Everyone has laid things down and had them disappear. Sometimes they turn up and sometimes they do not—the fourth dimension, perhaps.

I met Mr. Patton the next evening as he had arranged. He fell into step beside me.

"How's it going?" he asked.

"I'm learning to be a first-rate lady's maid," I said, rather peevishly, I am afraid. "I massage, manicure, and give scalp treatments, and I've got a smirk from trying to look cheerful. The experiment is a failure, Mr. Patton. I'm not nursing, for there's no real illness, and I'm not helping you any. And the dreadful decorum of the house gets me. If I were twenty, I'd run away, too. Nothing ever gets dusty or out of place. No door ever slams. When I raise a window for air, I put in a gauze-filled frame to keep the dirt out!"

"Has the mother talked at all?"

"All the time—about herself. I've learned a little, of course. The girl has been moody—would not let Mr. Plummer, her fiancé, visit her this summer. Seemed to be in trouble, but confided in no one. The family relationships seem to have been all right. They adore her."

"Have you seen many of the people who come and go about the house—intimate friends and relatives?

"Nearly all, I think."

"Anyone who could answer the description of the man she met at the station—the light-haired chap?"

I considered.

"None, I am sure."

"She and her mother got along well?"

"I think so. They were always together."

"Is there any trace of another love affair?"

"Yes, she was engaged once before. To a Mr. Wilson Page. She broke the engagement herself."

That interested him. He said he would look up Mr. Page.

"And don't be impatient," he advised me. We had made our circuit of the block and were in sight of the house again. "These are long cases sometimes—but the longer the time, the more sure I am that the girl is alive. Murder will out; it's self-limiting, like a case of measles. But take a girl who wants to stay hidden, and if she's intelligent, there's hardly any way to locate her. How many servants in the house?"

"Seven, I believe."

"Keep an eye on them. If one of them is garrulous, let her talk. They know more of the family than any member of it."

This brought to my mind the curious episode of the old woman, and I told him about it. He listened without interruption.

"When you say old, how old?"

"Seventy, I should say. She was stooped—and rather lame, but very active."

"You are sure you saw her? You could not possibly have been dozing?"

"I was making coffee; I don't customarily do that in my sleep. I think it must have been the cook. She is the only servant I have not seen. And, as to dozing, does anybody dream a handbag with straps and buckles?"

He put a hand on my arm impressively.

"It may interest you to know," he said, "that the cook is a young woman; I interviewed her myself. There is no person such as you describe in the house!"

"But why—at three in the morning—"

"Exactly," he said dryly. "Why? That's for us to find out."

He got a careful description of the old woman from me, and an account of her exit by the French door from the dining room into the garden. He was excited, for him, and rather triumphant.

"Now was it a mistake to put you there?" he demanded. "Of course not! And the next thing is to find the old lady. You can help there. Tell your story to the family. Set them to wondering and guessing. They may place her for us at once. In this business, try direct methods whenever you can. They save time."

He left me at the corner, and I went on alone. Just before I reached the house, a man ran down the steps and went away rapidly. The parlor maid was just closing the door.

"Did that gentleman inquire for me, Mimi?" I asked. "I am expecting my brother." I was learning!

"No, miss. He asked for Miss March." Her eyes were wide and excited. "When I said she was not here, he ran down the steps in a hurry."

"My brother," I persisted, "is short and dark. Perhaps you—"

"He asked for Miss March," she repeated. "And, anyhow, he was thin and lightish." She turned to see whether any of the family might overhear. "He's been here before, Miss," she confided, lowering her voice. "Twice, in the last week. He—he isn't one of Miss March's friends—I know that. And tonight he left this."

She showed me her tray on the hall table. There was a note on it addressed: "Miss Clare March. Important."

"I'll take this up to Mrs. March, Mimi," I said. "And if he comes again, ask him in and call me."

"Call you, miss?"

"Call me," I said quietly. "When he asks for Miss March, merely ask him to come in. Then call me. Mrs. March has requested me to see him."

I took the letter and went upstairs, but I did not give it to Mrs. March at once. That night, while I made my coffee, I steamed open the envelope and read the contents. It was on pale lavender paper and was as follows:

I implore you to see me as soon as posible. Come to the old place. I am up against it for sure. Don't let this go any longer! It's life or death with me!

I made a careful copy of the note, even to the misspelled word, and sealed it again. Mr. March was out that night—a girl had been found in a hospital. He was always following some such forlorn hope, returning each time a little sadder, a little grayer.

Mrs. March was unusually exacting the next morning. She wakened at dawn with a cry and I went to her. I was sleeping on the couch at the foot of the bed. She was sitting up, terrified, in the gray dawn. She wailed that Clare needed her, was calling for her. She had heard her distinctly.

"Surely you do not believe in dreams!" I said sternly.

"Not in dreams, perhaps," she replied. She was still pallid. "But don't you think, Miss Adams, that people hear things in sleep that waking ears do not catch? You know what I mean. It's subconscious, or something."

"It's subnormal," I commented, and brought her back to earth with a cup of hot tea.

That morning, I gave Mr. March the note. We were at breakfast, and Mr. Plummer had dropped in, as he usually did, on his way to his downtown office.

Mr. March read it without comment and passed it to the other man. He was younger, less poised. I saw him change color.

"Who brought this?" he demanded.

"Mimi got it. It was left by a thin, fair-haired young man."

They called Mimi, but she knew no more than I had told them, except for one fact: She said the man had tried to push by her into the house and that he had insisted that Miss March was at home. They sent the girl out. They seemed to have no scruple about talking before me.

"It is mystifying enough," Mr. Plummer said. "Patton ought to see it. But it doesn't help much. Whoever wrote that did not know that Clare was— not at home."

"Thin and fair-haired!" repeated Mr. March. "That's what Patton said, Walter—about the man at the railroad station, isn't it?"

"Patton is a fool!"

I gathered that the idea of the fair-haired man was extremely distasteful to him. He was almost surly.

We were sitting at the small breakfast table in the bay. I thought it a good time to speak about the little old woman. Any lingering doubt I may have had as to her right to be where I had seen her was dispelled by their manner. They were abstracted at first, then interested, then astounded.

"But, my dear young woman," Mr. March exclaimed, "why did you not rouse the house? And why did you wait for thirty hours before telling us?"

"It would be necessary for you to have seen her in order to understand. It never occurred to me that she was not a member of the household—she was so respectable. Only now, when I have seen all the servants, I begin to realize ... She went out through that door."

"Is anything missing?" Mr. Plummer asked. "Mrs. March's jewels?"

"Still in the safe-deposit vault. We have had no heart to think of them."

Nevertheless, a search of the house was made that day. Nothing was missing. Under Mrs. March's flushed directions, as she sat up in bed, I went round with great bunches of keys, verifying lists, looking up laces, locating furs. Such jewelry as she had about was safe.

As for the old lady with the jet on her bonnet, with the dolman and the buckled handbag—none of the family had ever known such a person. She answered no description, fitted into no place. Family and servants alike disclaimed her.

Life has a curious way of picking up threads and dropping them. The romantic young man with the blond hair, the little old lady with the limp, had come and gone, and for two weeks there was nothing more. Clare March remained missing. Mrs. March spoke of her in the past tense. Mr. Plummer grew thinner and took to coming into Mrs. March's room and sitting for long stretches without speech, his hands hanging listlessly between his knees.

I had my first real talk with Mr. Plummer late one afternoon while the invalid dozed in her chair. He was a good-looking man, something over thirty and already growing gray. He had sat for some time, apparently busy with his own thoughts—in reality watching me as I put away Mrs. March's various pretty trifles. She was always littered—ribbon bows, a nail file, a magazine, letters.

"Do you never make an unnecessary movement?" he asked at last.

"Frequently, I'm afraid."

"Must you put all those things away? Or will you sit down and talk for five minutes?"

I sat down near him. Mrs. March was now sound asleep.

"Do you want me to sit down and talk, or to sit down and listen?"

"To listen, and to answer some questions. Just a minute." He went quietly to the dressing table, returning with the photograph of Clare that stood there.

"You nurses know a lot about people," he said. "That's your business. You're a psychologist even if you don't realize it. I've watched you with Mrs. March. Now what do you read in that picture?"

"It is a lovely face," I replied, doing my best, but feeling utterly inadequate. Womanlike, I dare say I was anxious to say the thing he wanted to hear. "A— a pleasant face, I should say, but with character and temperament."

"What about the eyes?"

"They are well apart—that's a good sign, though cows are that way, aren't they! They are very direct and honest, too. Really, Mr. Plummer—"

"Here is a later picture, taken this summer. Now, what do you see?"

I was puzzled and uncomfortable.

"She looks older, more serious."

"Look at the eyes."

Well, there was a difference. I could not say where it lay. The effect was curious. In the early picture she was looking at the camera, and the eyes were limpid and clear. In the picture he had taken from his pocketbook, she gazed into the camera also, but there was a sort of elusiveness about the eyes. It gave me a strange feeling of indirectness, evasion—I hardly know what. They might have been the eyes of a woman who had lived hard and suffered. And yet this girl of twenty had hardly lived. It was almost a tragic face. I have seen the same drooping lines in eye cases, where vision is faulty and seeing an effort. What was this, then—astigmatism or evasion?

"You see it, don't you? Miss Adams, she has had some real trouble to make a change of that sort. I—I thought she was happy in our engagement, but as I look back, there are things—"

Mrs. March stirred and opened her eyes.

"I hate to waken," she said querulously. "It is only when I am asleep that I can forget, and even then, I dream. Go out now, please, Walter; Miss Adams is going to use the massager."

That afternoon at five o'clock Mr. Patton called me on the telephone for the first time.

"I think we have something," he said. "When you go out for your walk tonight, dress for the street. There will be a taxicab at the corner, and I shall be inside."

"At what time?"

"Seven thirty."

"Will an hour be enough?"

"Ask for two hours."

Mrs. March was rather peevish about my going out.

"I dare say you need air," she said, "but you could get it by opening a window. And what about my hot milk?"

"I'll ask Hortense to sit with you and she will heat the milk. I do not need air, of course. But I do need some exercise."

She let me go grudgingly. Mr. Patton would not tell me where we were going but insisted on talking of indifferent things. As it turned out, we were headed for a police station, and at last he voiced his errand.

"We are going to show you a lot of handbags," he said. "A woman pick-pocket was brought in here yesterday with four in a pocket under a skirt. I was looking over them today and it occurred to me that you might recognize one of them."

"Mine! I hope you send her up for a year!"

"Not yours. And do not jump to conclusions; it is fatal in this business."

I knew the bag at once when I saw it. Surely no other bag of that size in the city had two straps fastened with steel buckles. The handles of two of the other bags had been cut off, but the heavy leather handle of this one was entire.

"This is the one you mean, of course. Yes, it looks like the one the old lady carried, but there may be others. It is foreign, isn't it?"

"What was she doing that night when you noticed the bag?"

"She opened it and put in a pair of spectacles in a case."

He unfastened the bag and emptied onto a table a tin spectacle case, as quaint as the bag; two keys, one for a patent lock, the other an ordinary house key. Last of all, he drew from a pocket inside the bag a soiled and creased lavender envelope, stamped and ready for mailing. It was addressed in pencil to Mrs. March and had been opened. Mr. Patton drew out the communication inside and watched me as I read it. It was hardly decipherable and was written on a piece of wrapping paper:

"Am all right. Clare."

I stared at it.

"Interesting, isn't it?" commented Mr. Patton. "Did she write it or didn't she? If she's all right, why isn't she home? Why do all our little communications arrive in lavender envelopes? Who's the old lady? What was she doing in the house that night? What's the answer?"

"That could be the key to the garden door," I said dully.

IV

The doctor made a late call that night and dismissed Mrs. March as a patient.

"I'll drop in now and then to learn what the news is," he said as he prepared to leave. "You don't need me professionally. Just keep cheerful. It will all come out right."

I followed him into the hall. It seemed to me that if anyone knew the inside history I had failed to secure, it was he. And up to that time I had failed with him.

"I hope you will stay on, Miss Adams. I am leaving her in your hands—remember, no drugs so long as she is normal; at any symptoms of nervousness again, start them early."

"It's a trying case," I said slowly. "It takes it out of me, doctor. She asks me for theories, and—of course I didn't know the girl or her life—I cannot give her what she wants."

He hesitated. We were in the lower hall by that time.

"Just what does she want?"

"Encouragement."

"That Clare is living, of course. Well, tell her this the next time she is down. It is true enough. Tell her Clare was unhappy in her engagement and that I believe there is another man, that she has eloped with him, and that her message to the family has miscarried."

"Wilson Page?"

He eyed me. For the first time, it occurred to me that he suspected my business in the house and that he was giving me information that ethically he would have refused.

"No; a blond fellow, rather thin. I have seen her meeting him in the park, and once I believe she met him in my reception room."

He seemed to regret this information the moment I had it and left immediately.

That night, after I had rubbed Mrs. March with coconut oil, used the massager, given her hot milk, and, finally, read her to sleep, I slipped into my room and sat down by the window. The autumn garden lay beneath, with no moon to bring out its geometrical desolation. And there, elbows on the sill, the chill air blowing about me, I tried to piece together the scraps I held: the little old lady, the blond man and his frantic note, the letter in the buckled bag. And again, I recalled the conversation Mr. Patton and I had had in the taxicab on our way back that evening.

"She's alive," he had said; "and she is in the city—if that note is hers, and I think it is. I'll show it to the father and the other chap in the morning. Then she is in hiding. Why?"

I lay down on a couch at the foot of Mrs. March's bed, but did not get to sleep, for some reason. The slightest movement of my patient found me wide-eyed and alert. Small sounds were exaggerated. A regular footstep that seemed to ascend the stairs for hours turned out to be a drip from a bathroom tap. The slow chiming of the hall clock set me crazy.

At two o'clock, I got up and went downstairs. In the waitress's pantry, off the dining room, there were beef cubes. It seemed to me that if I drank a cup of bouillon, I might sleep. As usual, the light was burning in the lower hall. The dining room was dark—I no longer required a night supper—and the little table in the bay window was bare. A street light beyond the garden showed the window and the longer rectangle of the garden door. I was not nervous.

I made my way through the unlighted dining room to the pantry, a small room, painted white, with a butler's slide, to the basement kitchen and a small white glass and silver refrigerator built into the wall, where the waitress kept the dining room butter and cream. The electric light was out of order there—I pressed the switch, but there was no answering flood of light. I had matches with me for the alcohol lamp, however, and found my bouillon cubes easily. Thus I was still in darkness when I opened the swinging door into the dining room.

Someone was trying the lock of the garden door! I do not mind saying I was terrified. The door was glass. To cross the room to the lighted hall would throw my whole figure into relief. I shrank back, breathing with difficulty, into my corner. Beyond the thin casement cloth of the door, I could see a moving shadow.

The lock did not give. It seemed to me, all at once, that I knew the silhouette—that here again was the little old lady, but now without her key. My heart ceased pounding. I was able to think, to calculate. I wondered whether she would break the glass. I planned to let her get in if she could and then to cut off her retreat by advancing on her from behind. I was very calm by that time—rather exalted, I dare say, at my own bravery. I put the packet of beef cubes into my pocket in order to have both hands free.

I do not know just when I realized that it was not the little old lady—I believe it was after one of the panes had been broken and had fallen with a soft crash onto the rug inside. The figure straightened; it was much taller than I had expected. I recall that my heart almost stopped and then raced on at a mad pace. I saw what I knew was a hand put through the opening; I heard the lock turn and the cautious opening of the door. The intruder was in the room with me.

Panic possessed me then. I turned wildly and threw myself headlong against the swinging pantry door. It was madness, of course. There was no exit from the little room, no way to fasten the door. I was in a cul-de-sac and in the black dark. I believe I opened a drawer and got a cake knife—at least, eons after, I found myself clutching one. I do not remember how I got it.

The swinging door remained undisturbed. When I could hear—above the pounding in my ears—there was no sound anywhere except the hall clock's slow chiming.

Many things I have never recalled clearly about that hideous night. I do not know, for instance, how long I stood at bay in the pantry; or how my courage rose from my knees, which ceased trembling, to my spinal cord, to my pulse, which went down from about a hundred and eighty, thin and stringy, to what I judged was almost normal, still irregular, but stronger. When my courage reached my brain, which was in perhaps fifteen minutes, though I would have sworn it was daylight by that time and I had stood there most of the night, I put my ear against the door and listened. There was no sound.

The instinct of my training asserted itself. Whatever was happening, my patient must not be alone. I must get up to the sickroom. In a few moments, it was an obsession. I must get back. My sense of duty was stronger than my terror.

I made the break at last, opening the door an inch or so. The room was quiet. With infinite caution I pushed the door farther open. I could see the room, solidly handsome, rather heavy, empty! I made my first few steps of progress with deliberate slowness. I knew that if I ran, panic would follow at my heels. I dared not look over my shoulder. Even the lighted hall brought small comfort, with the dark rooms opening off it, sheltering I knew not what. But I reached the foot of the stairs in safety. There I stopped.

A woman, dressed in rags, lay huddled on the bottom steps in a faint. She lay face down. Even when I had turned her over and had recognized the features of the photographs in the house, I was still incredulous. Nevertheless it was true. Bruised and torn, clad in rags, gaunt to the point of emaciation, Clare March had come home again.

It was the end of one mystery—the beginning of another.

V

My first feeling was one of horror. Her condition was frankly terrible. I even feared at first that she was dead. I found a pulse, however. I am big and strong; I got her down off the staircase and laid her flat on the floor. All the time, I was praying that none of the family or the servants had been roused. I did not want anyone to see her yet.

I brought down some aromatic ammonia and gave it to her in water. Mrs. March was sleeping calmly; across the hall, Mr. March also slept, audibly. I had a little time; I wanted an hour—maybe two.

She came to very gradually, throwing an arm over her head, moving a little, and finally opening her eyes. I talked soothingly to her.

"Now don't be alarmed," I said over and over. "You are at home, and everything is all right. I am a nurse. Everything is all right."

"I want—Julie," she said at last, feebly.

I had never heard the name.

"Julie is coming. Can you sit up if I hold you?"

She made an effort, and, by degrees, I got her into the music room, where she collapsed again; there being no couch, I put her down on the floor with a cushion under her head. Terrible thoughts had been running through my head. The papers had been full of abduction stories, and I confess I thought nothing else could explain her condition, her rags.

"I am hungry," she said when I got her settled. "I am—I am starving! I don't know when I have had anything to eat."

She looked it, too. I had the beef cubes in my pocket, and I left her there while I made some broth. I brought it back, with crackers. She was sitting in a chair by that time, and she drank the stuff greedily, blistering hot as it was.

I had my first chance to take an inventory of her appearance. It was startling. Her hands were abraded and blistered. She held one out to me pathetically, but without comment. Over one eye was a deep bluish bruise. Her face was almost colorless, and her forearm, where one sleeve had been torn away, was thin to emaciation. Every trace of beauty was eclipsed for the time. She was shocking—that is all.

Her clothing was thin and inadequate: a torn white waist, much soiled; a short, ragged black skirt; and satin bedroom slippers, frayed and cut. She had nothing on her head and no wrap, though the night was cold. She looked up at me when she held out the empty cup.

"How is Mother?"

"She has not been well. She is all right."

"Was it worry?"

"Yes. Do you think you can get up the stairs?"

"Is that all I am to have to eat?"

"I'll get more soon. You mustn't take too much at once."

She rose, and I put my arm around her. She had taken me for granted, childishly, but at the foot of the stairs, she halted our further progress to ask me, "Who are you? You are not a servant."

"I am a trained nurse. I've been caring for your mother during her illness."

We went up the stairs and into her room.

Mrs. March wakened about the time I had got the girl to her own room.

"Don't tell Mother yet," she begged. "Give me a little time. I—I'd frighten her now."

I promised.

When I went back, half an hour later, Clare had undressed herself and put on a negligee from the closet. She was sitting in front of the fire I had lighted, brushing out her hair. For the first time she was reminiscent of the girl of the photographs. She was not like them yet—she was too gaunt.

I tried to coax her to bed, but she would not go. I was puzzled. Her nervous excitement was extreme; more than once she stopped, with brush poised, as if she were on the point of asking me some question; but she never asked it—her courage evidently failed her. It was a horrible night. I sat inside the door of my patient's room, in darkness, and watched the door opposite. I could hear the girl pacing back and forth; I was almost crazy.

I offered her a bromide, which she refused to take. But about half past three, I heard her lie down on the bed, and some of the tension relaxed. I had a chance to think, to work out a course of action. Mr. Patton should be notified at once, and as soon as the girl was really composed, I would rouse Mr. March. I knew I would be criticized in the family for not rousing them all at once, but I am always willing to take the responsibility for what I do—the doctor's orders first and my own judgment next is my motto. And there have been times when the doctor's orders—but never mind about that.

I looked at my watch. It was almost four o'clock and still black dark. I went down to the library, where the telephone stood on a stand behind a teakwood screen, and called up Mr. Patton's apartment, but I could not get him.

I hung up the receiver and sat there in the darkness, meaning to try again in a moment or so. It was while I was still there that I heard Clare on the stairs.

She came slowly and painfully—a step; a pause for rest, another step. Once down in the lower hall, she made better progress. She came directly into the library, through the music room, and turned on the lights.

I was curious. It was easy to watch her through the carved margin of the screen. It was only curiosity. I had no idea there would be further mystery to solve. In the morning, she would tell her story, the law would take hold, and that would be all. But I recall distinctly every movement she made.

First, she went to the long table littered with magazines, with the bronze reading lamp in the center.

She glanced over the magazines as they lay, picked up the framed picture of herself, and looked at it for a long moment, her hands visibly trembling. Then she took a survey of the room.

There was an English fender about the fireplace, with a tufted leather top. Mr. Plummer habitually sat there, with his back to the fire. And just inside, thrown carelessly, lay a newspaper. It was the newspaper she wanted. It was not easy for her to reach it in her weakened condition. She stooped, staggered, bent again, and got it.

The wood fire had burnt itself out, but the warm bricks and ashes still threw out a comforting heat. She curled up on the floor by the fender and proceeded to go over the pages, running a shaking finger through paragraph after paragraph. I was most uncomfortable, half ashamed, and cramped from my position.

When I felt that I could stand no more, she found what she was looking for. I heard her gasp and then saw her throw herself forward, her face in her arms, crying silently but fiercely, her shoulders shaking. She paid no attention when I bent over her, except to draw herself away from my hand. When I tried to take the newspaper, however, she snatched it from my hand and sat up.

"Go away!" she said hysterically. "Stop following me and watching me. Can't I even cry alone?"

I was rather offended. I drew back, like a fool, and lost a clue that we did not find until weeks later.

"I'm sorry you feel that way," I said coldly and went out and up the stairs.

She burned the paper before she made a laborious and faltering ascent of the staircase half an hour later—at least, when I went down, there was no sign of it or of any of the newspapers that had littered the room. And, though Mr. Patton secured copies of them all later and we went over them patiently, we could find nothing that seemed to have the remotest bearing on what we were trying to learn.

She was much better by morning—had slept a little; was calmer; had a bit of color in her ears, which had been wax-white; but the bruise on her forehead was blacker.

I broke the news of her return very gently to Mr. March at dawn and left it to him to tell his wife. I went to her afterward and found her hysterically impatient to see her daughter. I induced her to wait, however, until she had had an egg and a piece of toast. I do not believe in excitement on an entirely empty stomach. We covered the bruise with a loop of Clare's heavy hair; then her father and mother went in, and I closed the door.

Somebody had telephoned for Mr. Plummer, but she sent her father out to say she would not see him just yet. It was like a blow in the face. He almost reeled.

"That's the message, boy," Mr. March said. "I don't understand it any more than you do. She's in frightful condition; we've sent for the doctor. Tomorrow, I am sure—"

"But what does she say?" Mr. Plummer broke in. "Where has she been? I'll wait until she wants to see me, of course, but for God's sake tell me where she has been!"

"She has told us very little," Mr. March had to confess. "She is hardly coherent yet. She says she will talk to the police sometime today. She has been imprisoned—that is all we know."

Mrs. March's sitting room was open, and Mr. Plummer went in and sat down heavily. Sometime later, as I passed the door, he called me in.

"You saw her first, didn't you?" he asked. "Will you sit down and tell me all you know about it?"

I was glad to talk—I had been bottled up for so long. I told him everything—except my reason for being down in the library behind the screen.

"Did she ask for me at all?" he asked when I had finished.

"I—I think so. Naturally she would."

He smiled at me wryly.

"You know she did not ask for me," he said and got up.

I was very sorry for him. He was so earnest, so bewildered. He waited round all morning, hoping for a message, and about noon she said she would see him. Her own maid dressed her and together we put a little rouge on her face and touched up her color-less lips. Except for the hollows in her cheeks, she looked lovely. I gave her message to him.

"Tell him I want to see him," she said to me; "but he is not to ask a lot of questions, and he is to stay only a minute or two—I am so very tired."

He was uncertain of his welcome, I think. I took him to the door. She was on a couch, propped up with pillows, and the bruise was covered. And when I saw the look in his eyes and the assuring flame in hers, I knew that, whatever else was wrong, it was nothing that lay between them. The vision of the blond man as Clare's lover died at that moment and never came to life again.

The story of the almost two months of Clare March's disappearance she told to Mr. Patton that afternoon. She would not allow her father and mother to be present, and only Mr. Patton's insistence that the nurse should be there to see that she did not overtax her strength secured my admission. The story was short and was told haltingly. It gave me the impression of truth, but of being only a part of the truth. Her descriptions of the people and of the surroundings, for instance, were undoubtedly drawn from painful memory. They were photographic—raw with truth. The same was true of her story of the escape.

"It was on the third of September that you started home," Mr. Patton said. "We know that, and that you arrived on the morning of the fourth. We lost you from the time you got into a taxicab at the station. Did you order the man to drive you home?"

"Not directly. I went to—" She named the department store to which she had been traced. "I had made my purchase when a young man came up to me and introduced himself. He said I did not know him, but that he was living in the same house with an old German teacher of mine, Fräulein Julie Schlenker. She had taught me at boarding school and I was very fond of her. He said she was—dying."

Tears came into her eyes. Mr. Patton caught my eye for the fraction of a second.

"Was this before you bought the blankets or after?"

She looked startled, but he was smiling pleasantly. If she had to reassemble her story, she did it well and quickly.

"Before. I was terribly worried about Julie," she said. "I agreed to go there at once, and I asked him what I could take her to make her comfortable. He said she couldn't eat, but perhaps blankets—or something like that. I bought blankets and had them put in the taxicab."

"What address did this blond young man give you?"

"I did not say he was a blond young man," she objected. "I do not remember what he looked like. I should not know him again."

Mr. Patton nodded gravely.

"My mistake," he said. "Was this the same taxicab?"

"No; I had dismissed the other. I got into the taxicab, and the man gave an address to the driver. I paid no attention to it. I was upset about Julie. I hardly looked out. We went very fast. All the time I was seeing Julie lying dead, with her poor old face—" She shuddered. Clearly that part of the story was true enough and painful. "We drove for a long time. I was worried about the bill. When the register said four dollars I was anxious. I had checks, but very little money."

She stopped herself suddenly and gave Mr. Patton a startled glance, but he was blandness itself.

"Four dollars!" he said. "Did you know the neighborhood?"

"Not at all. I was angry and accused the driver of taking a roundabout way. He said he had gone directly and offered to ask a policeman."

"You were still in the city then?"

"Yes, but it was far out. When the driver drew up, I had just enough money to pay him. It was almost five dollars."

"Can you remember exactly?"

"Four dollars and eighty cents. I gave that man five dollars. I had only a dollar left."

"The young man was still with you?"

"No, indeed. I was quite alone. I wish you would not interrupt me."

Mr. Patton sat back good-humoredly and folded his hands. I knew why he had continually broken in on the story. I thought he had caught something, by his look.

"I got out. I had the blankets and they were bulky. The man carried them to the doorstep and drove away. I thought it was a queer neighborhood. It was a mean little house, off by itself, with only an unoccupied house near.

"I felt very strange, but Julie was always queer.

"I asked for Julie. A hideous old woman answered the door. The whole place was filthy. I felt terribly for Julie—she was always so neat. I went in and up the stairs. The stairs were narrow and steep and shut off below with a door. All I could think of was Julie in that horrible place. There were cobwebs along the stairs. We turned toward the back of the house and stopped before a door. The old woman did not rap. She opened it and said, 'In here, miss.' I went in. The room was empty. I said, 'Why, where is Julie?' But the old woman had gone. I heard her outside locking the door."

That was a strange story we listened to that afternoon—a story of futile calls for help; of bread and water passed through a broken panel in the door; of a drugged sleep, from which she wakened to find her clothing gone and rags substituted; of drunken revels below; and of the constant, maddening surveillance through the panel by a man with a squint. She described the room with absolute accuracy and even drew it roughly for Mr. Patton: a low attic room with two small windows; a sloping roof;

discolored plaster from a leak above; a washstand without bowl or pitcher; for light, a glass lamp with a smoked chimney; and for furniture, a cot under the lowest part of the ceiling and a chair.

Once a day, she said, the old woman brought her a tin basin for washing, and a towel, rough-dried. The basin had a red string to hang it up by, she said. The towels were checked—pink and white.

"Like glass towels," she said. "There was a grate for coal and a wooden shelf above it, with an old steel engraving tacked up on the wall. One corner was loose, and if I left the window open, it flapped all the time. I had a fire only once, but I did not suffer from cold—the kitchen was beneath, and the flue was always warm."

"This steel engraving—do you remember what it was?"

"The Landing of the Pilgrims," she said promptly. "Someone had colored a part of it with crayons—a child probably."

Mr. Patton looked puzzled. She might have invented the panel in the door or the man with the squint, but parts of her story bore the absolute imprint of truth: the chimney flue being warm, the flapping picture, the rough-dried towels, the basin with a red string through its rim.

"In a moment, I want you to tell us how you got away," Mr. Patton said, "but first—I want a reason for all this. Was it—did they try to force you to anything?"

"Nothing at all."

"They were not white slavers then?"

She colored. "No."

"They never threatened you?"

She hesitated, considered.

"Only when I cried out—and that did no good. There was only an empty house near."

"Miss March, this is an almost incredible story. A crime must have a motive. You are saying that you were imprisoned in an isolated house for nearly two months, were unharmed and unthreatened, but under constant surveillance, and finally made your escape. And you can imagine no reason for it!"

"I haven't said that at all—I imagined plenty of reasons. Couldn't they have wanted a ransom?"

"They made no attempt to secure one."

She told of her escape rather briefly. If I can give in so many words my impression of her story, it was that here and there she was on sure ground, and that the escape was drawn absolutely from memory and was accurate in every detail.

"Every now and then, they all got drunk," she said. "I—I always thought they would set the house on fire. The two younger women would sing—and it was horrible."

"You did not say there were younger women."

She was confused.

"There were two. One was married to the man. They called the old woman Ma. And there was a man with a wooden leg who visited the house. He came over the field; I saw him often. For two days they'd been drinking, and the old woman fell down and hurt herself. I could hear her groaning. And I was hungry—I was terribly hungry." She looked at me. "You know how hungry I was. I had not even water."

"She was starving," I said.

"Nobody came. I was frightened. I kept thinking that something had happened." She checked herself, started again. "All evening I lay in darkness. I could hear them yelling and singing, and now and then, the old woman groaning. And I was so thirsty I hoped it would rain and the roof would leak. That's how thirsty I was. I slept a little—not very much. Mostly I walked about and worried. The house was so quiet that it drove me crazy."

"Quiet! Were they asleep?"

She looked at him quickly.

"They went away—all of them. There was only the old woman, and she was hurt. When I called, nobody answered."

"How was your door fastened?"

"On the outside."

"Couldn't you have put your arm through the broken panel and unlocked it?"

"The key was not in the lock. It never was. It was always on a nail at the top of the staircase. I could see it."

No one could have doubted her. The key was kept at the top of the stairs on a nail. It takes a perceptible second to invent such a detail. She had not invented it.

"All the next day, no one came near me. One of the windowpanes was broken. I called through it for help. Sometimes there were people in the fields beyond the house. There was nobody that day except some little boys. They paid no attention; perhaps they did not hear me. I was getting weaker all the time. I thought that pretty soon I would be too weak to try to escape. The fire was out below and my room was cold. My hands were so stiff I could hardly move them. I worked a long time at the window. They had driven nails in all round it. I worked them loose."

She held out her hands. They were cut and blistered.

"I got them out at last, but I broke a pane of glass. I hardly cared whether it was heard or not. I had never been able before to see what lay below the window. There was a sort of shed there.

"I had to wait until night. The room was freezing, with the window out. They were still away, except the old woman. She lay and groaned down below. I lay on the mattress the rest of the day and shivered. As soon as it was dark, I crawled up on the windowsill. I was frightened—it looked so far down. I lowered myself by my hands and then dropped, but I slipped. I thought I had broken my ankle. The loose boards on the shed made a frightful noise."

"How did you find your way home?"

"I walked for hours. I do not know anything about the streets. I just walked toward the glow of the city lights against the sky. When I got into the city proper, I knew where I was."

"Where were you when you first recognized your surroundings?"

"I saw the North Market."

"Do you remember from which direction you approached it?"

"The west side, I believe." Her tone was reluctant.

Mr. Patton drew a soiled lavender envelope from his pocket and took out its enclosure.

"Am all right. Clare," he read. "Now, Miss March, just when and where did you write this little note?"

Her only answer was to break into hysterical crying. "Julie! Julie!" she cried. She absolutely refused to explain the note. It was an impasse. She could neither explain it nor ignore it. She took refuge in tears and silence.

That was the end of Clare March's story. It sounded like madness, but there was proof of a sort—her general condition; her hands; her brief but photographic descriptions. It was true—at least in part. It was not the whole truth. She had not spoken of the blond man or of the little old lady in black, and yet I was convinced she knew about them both. Mr. Patton thought as I did, for when she was quieter, he asked for a description of the old woman of her story.

"She was very stout," she said slowly, "and very dirty. She always wore the same things—a blue calico dress and an apron. She seemed to be washing all the time; the apron was always wet and soapy. And she had thin gray hair drawn into a hard knot."

"Could you tell her nationality by her voice—her accent?"

"I'm afraid not."

"Did you ever see her dressed for the street?"

"Never."

"Then you never saw her in a black bonnet trimmed with jet and an old-fashioned dolman, and carrying a pocketbook fastened with two buckles?"

She leaned over suddenly and caught Mr. Patton by the wrist.

"I can't stand it any longer!" she cried. "What do you know? Was the paper wrong?"

When she saw by his face that he did not understand and could not help her, she sank back among her pillows. She would not answer any more questions and lapsed into a watchful silence.

VI

Naturally, I have never taken any credit for the solution of the Clare March mystery. Even now, when I am writing under an assumed name, I am uneasy. To be suspected would be my professional ruin. So far, I have been able to keep my double calling a profound secret. I may have been in your house. Think it over, those of you who have something to conceal—are you certain that the soft-walking, starched young woman to whom in your weakness you talked so freely—are you sure it was not myself? Under the skin, I said in the beginning—aye, and under the flesh and its weaknesses. Do you recall that day when you and a visitor talked at the bedside and I wrote letters in a corner by a window? How do you know but that your entire conversation, word by word, was at the Central Office in two hours? Did it ever occur to you before?

I wrote many letters that week. Mrs. March was up and about, bustling and busy; Clare was my patient. I no longer met Mr. Patton in the evenings. He was combing the outskirts of the city, I believe, and interviewing taxicab drivers. I sent a daily report to him by mail:

MONDAY—I notice one curious thing: She will not let me do much for her. Hortense, her maid, does some things—not much. She gets rid of us both whenever she can. I feel worse than useless. I have offered to give her massage, but she refuses. Mr. Plummer only comes to the door—she does not wish him to come in.

TUESDAY—Still weak and inert. A box of flowers every day from Mr. Plummer. I had once thought possibly she did not care for him, but today I saw her eyes again when she looked at the roses—I believe she is crazy about him. She would like to get rid of me, but her parents insist she needs me. Her hands are healing. There is one curious thing—her wrists are abraded. Did she say her hands were tied?

WEDNESDAY—The blond man has been here. I saw him from the stairs and went down. He is not what we thought at all. He is untidy and shabby. He was waiting inside the door, turning his hat round in his hands. I told him Miss March was ill, but he refused to leave. He said, "Tell her it is Samuels, and this is the last call. She'll know what I mean." I said, "I think she has had a letter from you." He turned livid. "Then she got it!" he stormed. "And she paid no attention to it! You tell her, for me, that she'll fix things with me now—today—or I'll tell the whole story!" He felt in his watch pocket and seemed to remember that his watch was gone. That added to his rage. "You tell her that. Tell her she'll have it at the old place by three this afternoon or I'll go to her precious sweetheart and tell him some things he ought to know." I tried to follow him when he left, but by the time I'd got my hat and ulster, he was out of sight. If Samuels is his real name, you can probably find him. He is blond and smooth-shaved, and has a gold tooth—right side, upper jaw; wears a tan overcoat and a soft green felt hat.

WEDNESDAY, four P.M.—I have just come back from an errand for Clare. I have been to the old place with a parcel for Samuels. It was money. He was so greedy that he tore it open while I waited. It seemed to be considerable—well over a hundred dollars. When he had counted it, he put it in his pocket. He looked better than in the morning and was calmer. He looked at me after he had counted it. "Don't look so damned virtuous!" he said. "This isn't blackmail. It's for value received."

The old place is at the corner of Tenth Street and the Embankment. We stood in the doorway of a vacant building and talked. Samuels looks decayed—as if he has seen better days. I tried to get you by telephone to follow me. You were out.

THURSDAY—A very curious thing happened to-day: Clare asked for some chicken cooked in cream. The cook had never done it, and I volunteered. It took some time; I was in the basement more than an hour. When I came up with the chicken, she had disappeared. We were all terribly frightened. I called the office twice, but you were out as usual—you will have to arrange some way for me to get you in emergencies. She had taken her wraps and gone out by the garden door. The parlor maid had not seen her. It was two hours later when she came back, exhausted. She locked herself in her room and it was almost the dinner hour before she would admit me.

Her father had a talk with her tonight. He said, "You must not do such unwise things. You will drive your mother frantic."

"Poor Mother!" she replied. "I'll tell you before long where I was. Don't ask me."

I thought she had been crying. I believe she has pawned or sold her sapphire ring; I do not see it.

That last letter, sent special delivery, and un-signed as all of them were, brought a telephone message from the detective and an appointment for that evening.

"Ask for an evening off," he said. "I think I've got it. And I want to talk to you."

He had a taxi at the corner that night. It was when it was well under way that he began to talk.

"We've got the house," he said. "The man with the squint did it—but that's a long story. In Miss March's anxiety to tell as much as she dared of the truth, she went a little too far. Given a four-dollar-and-eighty-cent taxicab radius, an isolated house with two young women, an old hag, and a man with a squint—put a shed on the back of the house and a bad reputation all over it—and you have perhaps two dozen possibilities. Add such graphic touches as a built-in stairway and a tin basin hung up by a red string as identification marks, and an empty house and a man with a wooden leg for neighbors, and out of the two dozen there will be one house that fits. We've found it."

"Is that where we are going?"

"To that neighborhood. I really wanted a chance to go over the whole thing with you. Now, then, what do you think? You've been close to the case—closer than I have. How much of that story of hers is true?"

"About half of it."

"Which half?"

"Well, I think she was not a prisoner. I believe she was a voluntary guest in the house she described and that she was hiding from something."

"I see. And not expecting us to find the house, she gave a circumstantial description. But what was she hiding from? So far as we can learn, her past has been an open book—she was away at school for four years and spent a year abroad with a party of girls and a chaperone. She came out two years ago—I remember reading about the coming-out ball, something very elaborate. That first winter, she went about with young Page, became engaged and broke it off. Page has been away ever since. It can't have anything to do with Page. Last spring, she took on this

Plummer—has been with her family all summer— has never, except during the year abroad, been away from her mother for any length of time. That doesn't look like anything to hide from. What do you think of the Julie story?"

"I don't believe it. But there is a Julie."

"Does the family know the name?"

"No. The girl is paying blackmail, Mr. Patton."

"The blond chap?"

"Yes."

"That was rotten luck, my being out of touch that day. If we had him—or if we had your friend, the little old lady!"

He stopped the taxicab shortly after, and we got out. We were well out of the center of town, in a scattering suburb. I had never seen it. And before us stretched one of those empty spaces that are left here and there, without apparent cause, during the growth of the city. House builders are gregarious—they build in clusters. Perhaps it's a matter of sewers or of gas and water. To right and left of us stretched a sort of field, almost bare of grass, with straggling paths across it. Long before, a street had been cut through; its edges were still intact—a pitfall for the unwary.

I did not see all this that night. It was late October and very dark. Mr. Patton had a pocket flash, and with that and his hand, I managed fairly. Our destination was before us—a little house, faintly lighted.

"I'm afraid this isn't very pleasant, Miss Adams," he apologized, "and I haven't a good reason for bringing you. But I'm up against it in a way. I want you to see this place and perhaps your instinct will tell you what I fail to make out. I've been here once today, and it stumps me. They swear they've never had a girl there; that the man with the wooden leg sleeps in the garret sometimes. He's a watchman at the railroad over there. By the way, did she speak of a railroad?"

"I think not."

"It's a bad place. The police protection doesn't amount to much, but over there in the town, they say it's a speakeasy. The cellar's full of beer. They say other things, too—that the old woman is a white slaver, for one thing. That bears out the story partly. And another thing does also—the hag hurt herself lately. She's going about with a cane. On the other hand—well, if they were lying today they did a good piece of work."

There was a wagon near the house as we approached. At first, we thought they were moving out. Then Mr. Patton laughed.

"Getting rid of the beer and the empties," he said. "Got them scared! Now don't be nervous. You needn't speak to them. I want you to keep your eyes open—that's all."

I was nervous. There was something sinister about the very location. I have even now rather a hazy recollection of Mr. Patton's rap at the door, the imperious summons of the law, and of a hideous old woman who peered out into the darkness.

"Well, Mother," Mr. Patton said cheerfully, "here I am again. I want to look round a little."

The hag made as if to close the door, but a woman spoke from behind.

"Let him in, Ma," she said. "We ain't got nothing to hide. Come in, mister."

A man came up from the cellar with a box of bottles. I can still see his face over the bottles—his sickening pallor, his squint. He thought it was a raid, clearly. Then he saw me and his color came back.

"I guess a man's 'ouse is 'is own," he snarled. "We drink a little beer ourselves. That ain't agin' the law, I reckon."

"Not at all," Mr. Patton said good-humoredly. "I'll have a lamp, please."

It appeared to be a four-roomed house. We stood in the front room, an untidy place with a bed in a corner, and heavy with stale odors. Behind, there was a kitchen containing a table littered with the remains of the evening meal. Between the two rooms was a narrow, steep staircase shut off with a door below and ending above in a small landing. From this landing two doorways opened—one into a front room, the other into a half room, or attic, over the kitchen. It was into this room that Mr. Patton, carrying a smoky lamp, led the way.

"This is the room," he said. "That is the window with the shed below. Here is where the flue comes up from the kitchen."

I looked round. It was a sordid, filthy place. The plaster had broken away here and there. Where it was intact, it was discolored from a leaking roof. For furniture, there was a mattress on the floor, with soiled bedding, a chair with a broken seat, and a washstand. Clare had said the washstand was unfurnished, but had mentioned a tin basin. Here was a tin basin with a red string. Mr. Patton was watching me grimly.

"Well, what do you make of it?" he said.

"It looks queer," I admitted. "Only there are some things—the panel in the door, for instance. There is no door."

"I asked about that. They say it came off the hinges a month or so ago and they chopped it up for firewood."

I was still looking about. He had stooped and was examining the door hinges.

"She said she broke the glass. One window is broken, but this one over the shed is not."

He came over and ran his hand over the window frame.

"Sash is nailed in, which I believe was also mentioned!" he said. Our eyes met in the dim light—a friendly clash; he was so sure of the place and I was so doubtful.

As I stood there peering into the squalid corners of the attic, I remembered the daintiness of the girl's room at home—its bright chintz and shining silver, its soft lamps, its cushions, its white bath beyond. I remembered the exquisite service of the March household and tried to picture the hag below climbing that ladder of a staircase with a platter of greasy food. I tried to forget Clare in her lovely negligee and to recall the haggard creature who had dropped in her rags at the foot of the staircase. And I tried to place the wretched girl of that night in this wretched place. I could not do it. There was something wrong.

Mr. Patton turned to me, gravely smiling.

"Now, then, your instinct against my training," he said. "Is this the place?"

"I do not believe she was ever here," I said. "Don't ask me why—I just don't believe it." But a moment later I felt that my instinct had received a justification. "Do you remember," I said, "a graphic description of a steel engraving that flapped in the wind?"

"By George!"

"There is not only no engraving—there are no nail holes in the plaster. There has never been such an engraving here," I said in triumph.

VII

I have often wondered what would have happened had we taken Clare March the next day to that untidy house in Brickyard Road. Brickyard Road was the local name of the street that had been cut through and forgotten.

Would she have told the real story or not? If not, how would she have explained the discrepancy, for instance, of the missing engraving? Would she have taken refuge in silence? Had she hoped by the very detail of her description to throw us off the track? Did she wonder, those dreadful days, how the bag with the buckles had come into the hands of the police and yet had not led us further? Did she suspect me at any time?

Sometimes I thought she did. She would not let me do much for her. I gave her the medicines that were ordered, saw to her nourishment, read to her occasionally. Her own maid looked after her personally. It rather irritated me. More than once, I found her watching me. I would glance up from my book and find her eyes on me with a question in them, but she never asked it.

Mr. Patton was waiting eagerly to take her out to Brickyard Road, but she was still very weak, and she showed a distaste for the excursion that was understandable enough under the circumstances. Other things puzzled me, however—her unwillingness to see Mr. Plummer was one. Yet she sat for hours looking at his picture. I suspected, too, that her maid was closely in her confidence. More than once, I caught a glance of understanding between them. Sometimes I wondered if Clare was quite normal—not insane, of course, but with some queer mental bias.

Outwardly, everything was calm. She lay or sat in her fairylike room, with flowers all about her. Her color was coming back. In her soft negligees, she looked flowerlike herself. The picture was quite complete: a lovely convalescent, a starched and capped nurse, a maid in black and white, flowers, order, decorum, with a lover hovering in the background. But the nurse was making notes on her record that were not of symptoms, the maid was not clever enough to mask her air of mystery, and the lover paced back and forth downstairs waiting for a word that never came.

On the day following my excursion with Mr. Patton, going into my own room unexpectedly, I found Hortense, the maid, in my clothes closet. She made profuse apologies and backed out. She had been looking, she said, for a frock that had been mislaid. I did not believe her.

After she had gone, I made a careful examination of the closet. A row of my white linen dresses hung there, my street clothes, my mackintosh. In a far end, where I had placed them the night she arrived, were the ragged garments in which Clare had come home. I locked my door and, taking them out, went over them carefully.

There was a worn black skirt, rather short, a ragged and filthy waist of poor material and carelessly made, put together by hand with large stitches and coarse thread. The undergarments were similarly sewed. They might have come from just such a place as the house in Brickyard Road. The skirt was different. Though ragged, it was well made, and it had been shortened. It had been altered at the top, too, I decided—the belt taken off and put on again inside out.

I found something just then. On the inside of the belt was woven the name of one of the leading tailors in the city. I thought that over awhile. The skirt could hardly belong to Brickyard Road. It seemed to me that this was a valuable clue. It seemed to me that Hortense knew this also, and that there was no time to be lost.

The situation was put up to me that day in an unexpected fashion. Mr. Patton slipped on the first ice of the season and injured the leg that had been hurt before. He was almost wild with vexation.

"Just keep wide awake," he wrote me by special delivery, "and send me the usual daily bulletins. If anything very important happens, come round and see me. The people we saw are being watched. If you meet the blond chap, follow him until you get a chance to telephone. I'll send someone to relieve you. We haven't got it all yet by any means."

It rather knocked my plans, especially as I could tell by the shaky writing that he was suffering when he wrote the letter. It seemed to me that for a day or so I should have to get along alone.

But I could do something—I could perhaps trace the skirt.

I had been in the March house now for eight weeks and had had practically no time off. When I asked for two hours, Mrs. March offered me the remainder of the day.

I took it; I was glad to get it.

I took the skirt along, carrying it out quite calmly under Hortense's not too friendly eyes. I thought it probable she would miss it, but I could see no other way. I wanted to identify the skirt. If it had been made for Clare, her story of having had all her clothing taken away from her would fall to shreds. If it had not, I meant to trace it. And trace it I did that autumn afternoon, while the dead leaves in the park made crackling eddies under the trees, while the wind held me back at every corner, while fashionable women donned the first furs of the season and sallied forth to the tailors for their winter garments. I, too, went to a tailor.

I dare say I was not fashionable enough to be worthwhile. It was a long time before I received attention, and my few hours were flying. When at last the manager turned to me, I indicated my bundle.

"I want to trace a skirt that was made here," I began. "Your name is on the belt. It is very important."

"But, madam," he said, "we cannot give any information that concerns our customers."

"This is vitally important."

"It would be impossible. We turn out a great many costumes. We keep no record of the styles."

"There is a number on the belt."

I believe he suspected me of divorce proclivities. He held out both hands, palms up.

"Madam surely understands—it is impossible!"

I turned over the lapel of my coat and he saw a badge that Mr. Patton had given me. He had said, "Don't use it unless you need to, but when the time comes, flash it!"

I flashed it. I got my information within ten minutes, but it did not help at first. He gave me the name of the woman for whom it had been made. I had never heard of her—a Mrs. Kershaw.

"You are quite positive?"

"Positive, madam. The number is distinct. Also, one of the skirtmakers recalls—it was part of a trousseau a year or so ago."

A sort of lust of investigation seized me. I had started the thing and I would see it out. With a new deference, the tailor handed me my rewrapped bundle and saw me to the door.

"No trouble with the Kershaws, I hope?" he said.

"None whatever," I answered at random. "She gave a skirt away and I am tracing it."

That was it, of course. I said it first and believed it afterward. She had given the skirt away.

It took an hour and a half of my shortening afternoon to locate and interview Mrs. Kershaw. She was quite affable. I did not show my badge—it was not necessary. I made up a story about some stolen goods, with this skirt among them. She was anxious to help, she said, but . . .

"I hardly remember," she said. "I gave away a lot of my wedding clothes—the styles changed so quickly. Why, I remember exactly what I did with that! I gave it to the Fräulein—Fräulein Schlenker. But stolen goods! She's the most honest old soul in the world."

"She is old then?"

"Oh, yes—quite. Such a quaint little figure. She taught me at boarding school; she seemed old even then. Poor Fräulein Julie!"

My lips were dry. Julie!

"Would you mind describing the Fräulein, Mrs. Kershaw?"

"You do not suspect her of anything?"

"No, indeed, but I should like to find her."

"Well, she is a little thing, stooped and lame. She hurt her ankle after I first knew her. She is very saving—we all thought she was rich—but I believe not. There's a brother, or someone, that she helps. She wears a rusty black bonnet with jet on it, and a queer old wrap, and—oh, yes—she always carries the same bag—a foreign one, with buckles. I really think the bag was the reason we thought she was wealthy. It seemed such a secure affair."

Julie, then, was my little old lady of the dining room and the garden door! And there was more than that—the school was the school from which Clare had graduated.

"Have you seen the Fräulein lately?"

"We have been away all summer. She may have called. I'll ask."

The little old lady had not called, however. I got her address. It seemed to me that things were closing up.

It was quite dark when I left the Kershaw house. It was very cold and I was hungry, but excitement would not let me eat. I was getting my first zest for this new game I was playing, and I was losing my shrinking horror of spying into affairs that were not my own. It seemed to me that my cause was just, for if Clare March had not been incarcerated in the Brickyard Road house, she might still, out of terror of the truth, insist that she had been. Hysterical young women had done such things before. I held no brief

for the family in Brickyard Road, but if they were
innocent, they were not to suffer. I was after the
truth, and I felt that I should get it. I had no course
of action mapped out. I wanted to confront the little
old lady—I got no further.

It was seven o'clock when I reached the house. I
had crossed the city again. I was hungry and shiver-
ing with cold, and I still carried the parcel under my
arm. For the first time that day, I was nervous. The
fear of failure assailed me. I used to have the same
feeling when I had charge of the operating room and
a strange surgeon was about to operate. Would he
want silk or catgut? What solutions did he use?
Would the assistant get there in time to lay out the
instruments? So now with the Fräulein—would
she deny the skirt? If she did, should I accuse her
of the night visit to the March house? Or of the
letter in the buckled bag?

The house was a small one on a by-street, a
comfortable two-story brick, with a wooden stoop
and a cheerful glow through the curtains of a vestibule door. The woman who answered my ring was
clearly the mistress. She wore a white apron and there
was an agreeable odor of cooking food in the air.

"Fräulein Schlenker?" she said. "Yes; she made
her home here. She is not here now."

"Can't you tell me where I may find her?"

She hesitated.

"I don't know exactly. We've been anxious about her lately. She went away for a vacation about two months ago. Did you want to see her about renting the house in Brickyard Road?"

For just a minute, I distinctly saw two white aprons and two vestibule doors!

"Yes," I said as coolly as I could. "When—when will it be empty?"

"It is empty," she replied. "I hardly know what to do. She's been anxious to rent it, but now that she's away and no word from her ... Would you like the key?"

The empty house in Brickyard Road!

"If I might have it."

"You'll return it soon, won't you?" She went into the hall and got a key from the drawer of a table. "She'll do anything that's reasonable—paper the lower floor and fix the roof. It's a nice little house." I took the key, still rather dazed. "It's a growing neighborhood out that way," she went on, evidently eager to do her roomer a good turn. "Some of these days, that street will be paved." She had an air of doubt; she was clearly divided between eagerness and trepidation. "You'll be sure to return the key?"

"I'll have it back here tomorrow."

She watched me down the street, still vaguely uneasy. I tried to make my back honest, to step as one who walks the straight and narrow path. I had a feeling that she might suddenly change her mind and pursue me, commanding the return of the key. I hardly breathed until I had turned the corner.

I got something to eat at the first restaurant I saw. I needed food and time to think. I meant at first to telephone Mr. Patton. As I grew warmer and less fatigued, I decided to go on alone. It was my first case; I wanted to make good—frankly I desired Mr. Patton's approval, and something he had once said to me came back.

"In this business," he said, "there are times when two's a crowd." I remembered that.

I ate deliberately. I never hurry with my food—I've seen too many stomachs treated like coal cellars on the first cold day of fall. And as I ate, the key lay before me on the cloth. It had a yellow tag tied to it, endorsed in a small, neat script, very German.

"Key to the house in Brickyard Road," it said. "Kitchen door."

I had, at the best, about two hours and a half when I left the restaurant. That meant a taxicab. I counted my money. I had thirteen dollars. It would surely be enough.

Brickyard Road lay a square or two away from where I alighted. I retained the cab—out there in that potter's field of dead-and-gone real estate hopes, it was a tie with the living world. Its lamps made a comfortable glow. The driver was broad-shouldered. I borrowed a box of matches from him. I have often wondered since what he thought.

The house Mr. Patton and I had examined was dimly lighted, as before. I passed it at a safe distance. The empty house, that was the only other building in Brickyard Road, was my destination. The two houses were alike—clearly built by the same builder. Only the courage of an idea took me on. In the lighted house, the crone was singing—a maudlin voice. Someone was walking along the rickety boardwalk round the place—a step and a tap, a step and a tap— the one-legged man, of course.

There is something horrible about an empty house at night. A house is an intimate place; its every emanation is human. Life has begun and ended in it. Thoughts are things, I have always believed—things that leave their mark.

I had such a feeling about the little house in Brickyard Road. I was very nervous. The other house was near enough to be dangerous—too far away to be company. I felt terribly alone. There was not even starlight. I stumbled and fumbled along, feeling my way by the side of the house to the rear. There was a dispute going on next door. The crone had ceased singing. Someone broke a bottle with a crash.

I found the kitchen door at last. To reach it, I had to go through a wooden shed. In the safety of the shed, I struck a match and found the keyhole. The key turned easily. As I opened the door, a breath of musty air greeted me and blew out my match. The thick darkness closed down on me like a veil; I was frightened.

It was a moment or two before I could light a fresh match, and it took more than that for me to survey the kitchen. It had been in use not very long before. There was a kettle on the stove and a few odds and ends of dishes in orderly stacks on an up-turned box. And there was a loaf of bread, covered with gray-green mold. There was no table, no chair—only a cot bed, neatly made up, in a corner. I remember distinctly the comfort of discovering that orderly bed, with a log cabin quilt spread over it.

My match went out, but the box was almost full. I was not uneasy now. The peace of the log cabin quilt was on my soul. I found a smoky lamp with very little oil in it, and lighted it. My nerves are pretty good. I've laid out more than one body in the mortuary at night and alone. I was not going to be daunted by an empty house. Nevertheless, the glow of the lamp was comforting. I put down my bundle and went into the front room.

I had a real fright there. Something shadowy stood in the center of the room, moving very slightly. I almost dropped the lamp. I had a patient once who used to say her heart dropped a stitch. Mine did. Then I saw that it was a woman's black dress hanging on a gas fixture and moving in the air from the open kitchen door.

I began to feel uneasy. What if the house were inhabited? Certainly it had been occupied recently. I dare say I move softly by habit, but I doubled my ordinary caution. I wanted to get away, but I wanted more than that. I wanted desperately to see whether there was a steel engraving of the Landing of the Pilgrims in the attic room over the kitchen. If I was right—if in this house Clare March had been imprisoned—if her detail of the house next door was merely what she had gained from a window—what was the meaning of it all? Where was Julie? If I knew anything, this old black silk swaying in the air belonged to her.

Not, of course, that I reasoned all this out. I felt it partly, for the next moment I heard a door open at the top of the stairs. I blew out the lamp instantly, but a sort of paralysis of fright kept me from flight. I could have made it. The stairs, as in the house next door, were closed off with a door. A dash past this door, and I should have been in the kitchen. But I hesitated, and it was too late. The steps were at the lower door.

Now and then since that evening, I have a nightmare, and it is always the same. I am standing in a dark room and there are stealthy steps drawing nearer and nearer. At last, the thing comes toward me—I can hear it—but there is nothing to see. And then it touches me with ice-cold hands—and I waken with a scream. I frightened a nervous patient almost into convulsions once because of that dream of mine.

The darkness was terrible. Behind me the dress swayed, touched me. I almost fainted. The staircase door did not open immediately. I wondered frantic-ally what was standing and waiting there. It showed my abnormal mental condition when it occurred to me that perhaps the old woman, Julie—perhaps she was dead, and that this on the staircase was she again, come back. I almost dropped the lamp.

I braced myself against I knew not what when I heard the door opening. Whoever it was, was listening, I felt sure. Through the open kitchen door came the sound of singing from next door and of someone hammering on a table in time. It covered my gasping breaths, I dare say. The stair door opened wider, and someone stepped down into the tiny passage. We were perhaps eight feet apart.

I lived a century, waiting to hear which way the footsteps turned. They went toward the kitchen, still stealthily, with a caution that was more terrible than curses. I had a moment's respite then, and I felt my way toward the front door. If the key was there, I might yet escape. I found the door. The key was gone. Even in that moment of frenzy, I knew where the key was—in the buckled bag at the police station. I was trapped!

There were various sounds now from the kitchen: a match struck and a wavering search, probably for the lamp I held. Then a dim but steady light, as though from a candle, followed by the cautious lifting of stove lids and much rustling of paper. The paper reminded me of something—my bundle lay on the cot!

I knew the exact moment when it was discovered. I heard it torn open and I shivered in the silence that followed. Then the candle went out and there was complete silence again. But this time it was the quiet of strained ears and quickened senses. I dream of that, too, sometimes—of a silence that is a horror.

I dared not move a muscle. I felt that if I relaxed, I should stagger. I breathed with only the upper part of my lungs. Then, very slowly, there was movement in the next room—a step and then another. It was coming. While the light was burning, I had been terrified by something desperate, but at least quick with life. Now, in the darkness, it became disembodied horror again! It came slowly but inevitably, and directly toward me. I tried to move, but I could not. The black dress moved in the air; a chill breath blew on me. Then, out of the black void all round, a cold hand touched my cheek. I must have collapsed without a sound.

VIII

When I came to, I was lying on the floor of the empty room, with the black dress swaying above me. There was a faint light in the room. By turning my head, I saw that it came from the kitchen. Someone was moving quickly there; there was a rattle of china. A moment later, a figure appeared in the doorway and peered in.

"Are you awake, Miss Adams?"

It was Clare! I struggled to a sitting position and stared at her.

"Was it—you—before?" I asked.

"Yes. Don't talk about it just now. I have a fire going and soon we can have some tea. I think you are almost frozen—and I know I am."

It was curious to see how our positions had been reversed. And there was a change in Clare—she was almost cheerful. She helped me out into the kitchen and onto the cot, and then busied herself about the room.

"I am sure there is tea somewhere," she said, "Julie was always making tea."

She was dressed for the street—suit and hat and furs. She tried to make talk as she moved about the room, but the really vital things of the evening, she avoided. She fussed with the fire, filled the kettle afresh from a hydrant outside, rinsed out two cups, found tea, searched for sugar. And still, her eyes had not met mine.

She found me staring at an engraving that lay on the floor, however, and she dropped her artificial manner.

"The Landing of the Pilgrims!" she said gravely. "I was going to burn it."

The sounds in the next house died away. The kettle on the stove began to boil cheerfully. The little room grew bright with firelight. Clare drew the box before the cot and poured two steaming cups of tea.

"We will drink our tea," she said, "and then I shall tell you, Miss Adams. I am very happy tonight—I have only one grief."

What that was she did not say. She had found a
box of biscuits and opened it. She took very little
herself. She was plainly intent on making up to me
for my fright. She seemed to bear me no malice for
being there. It was not until I had drained my cup
that she put hers down.

"Now we'll begin," she said, and took off her
jacket. Next she drew up the sleeve of the soft
blouse she wore beneath and held out her arm for
me to see. I gave a shocked exclamation.

"Cocaine!" she said briefly. "The other arm is
also scarred. I got it first at school for toothache." I
could not say anything; I only stared. "But that's all
over now," she went on briskly. "Today I have—but
I'll tell you about that later. I knew there was only
one way out, Miss Adams—to do it myself. Father
and Mother would have helped me, of course, but it
would have been their will, not mine. I had to edu-
cate my own will to be strong enough. Oh, I'd
thought it all out. And then—I did not want them to
know. Even now, when I know it's over, I'm afraid to
have them know. I've lied to keep it from them, but
the detective knew it wasn't true."

She told me the whole story eagerly, frankly. It
was clearly a relief. She had made her plans that
summer and made them thoroughly. She had tried

before and failed. This time there was the great in-
centive—she wished to marry.

"I wanted to bring children into the world, Miss
Adams," she said. "I should not have dared—the
way things were. All summer, I tried and broke over.
I was almost crazy. Then I got a letter from Julie—
she had been my German teacher at school, and I
was fond of her. She had been taking care of an insane brother, who had died. She wanted to work
again. Poor Julie!

"I thought she could help me. I knew it would
be hard, though I didn't know—well, I wrote her the
whole story and told her my plan. I had been here to
see the brother with her; I knew the house. I asked
her to send out after dark for just enough to keep us
going for a time. I did not want the house opened. I
thought there would be a hue and cry, and they
might trace me to Julie."

"Your father and mother said they knew of no
one named Julie."

"They would have known of her as Fräulein
Schlenker. They had never seen her. I came to the
city, bought some blankets and a book or two, and
came out here. She was here and partly settled. She
was against the plan even then, but I showed her my
arms, and she knew I was desperate. I had a supply

of cocaine—I had got it in town. I was to have it—I should have died without—but she was to reduce the quantity. I locked myself in and gave her the key."

"You had been getting the cocaine from the man with the blond hair?"

"Yes. He was in a pharmacy at first—where I got the prescription filled. He suspected me after a time. After he lost his position, he still got it for me. I met him wherever I could—on the street, in the park, anywhere—but generally we met by the Embankment. He robbed me, I think. I owed him a great deal finally. He took to bothering me about it. I used up all my allowance and more.

"I gave Julie the cocaine. She was to reduce it a little at a time. I suffered the tortures of the lost, Miss Adams. But perhaps you know. There were many days when I wanted to kill myself. Once, Julie had to tie my hands behind my back. She was wonderful—wonderful! I owe it all to her. I was lost, Miss Adams. I would lie, steal, almost murder, to get the cocaine. I lived for it."

"All this was here in this house?"

"Upstairs—in the back room one window looked out over a field and could be kept unshuttered. I chose it. Besides, the fire from below heated it. We had only a little coal left in the cellar, and we could get none. Julie went out after dark and did our buying. It—it all took longer than I had thought. I planned for a month. It was more than that. We were running out of money. At the end of five weeks, we were desperate—and I sent Julie to the house."

I remembered that well enough! But I did not interrupt.

"Father always gave me the fees from directors' meetings, and, as they were in gold, I dropped them under the cushion of a silver box on my dressing table. Sometimes, there would be several; most of them went eventually to—to the man I spoke of. Before we went away in the summer, I had put some there; I could not remember how many—my mind was hazy—but I was sure there was perhaps fifty dollars. I had my own house keys with me, and I gave Julie the key to the garden door. She was terribly frightened, but we were desperate. She got in without any trouble and got it. There was forty dollars."

I remembered something. "Forty dollars and a book," I said, smiling.

"Forty dollars and a book—was it yours? The day came when she told me I had had no cocaine for a week. I was faint and dizzy, but I wrote a line to Father and Mother. I shouldn't have written it. It could never be reconciled with anything but the truth, and I was morbid about that. They were never to know. I did not want Mr. Plummer to know—I thought he would never trust me again. But I wrote it and Julie took it out. She never came back—and I was locked in, upstairs!"

"She never came back!"

"She was killed—struck by an automobile. I thought—didn't the detective know that? He had her bag."

So my little old lady was dead after all! I was sorry. What a spirit she had!

"I was locked in," Clare was saying. "I waited—and she did not come. I had not eaten for a day or so before, and there were two days and a night without even water. I was so desperate that I tried to call the other house, but the old woman had hurt herself, and there was no one about outside. I tried to break down the door. There was a panel in it—for the brother who was crazy. I could almost reach the key on the nail outside. The last day I think I was delirious. The key made faces at me through the panel. I told you, didn't I, about getting out of the window?"

"Yes. When did you learn about Julie?"

"The night I went home. As you know, I went down to the library and searched the newspapers. I felt that she had been hurt. As soon as I was strong enough, I slipped away from the house—they were going to give her a pauper's burial. I pawned a ring, and at least she did not have that."

She broke down, after keeping up bravely for so long. I gathered from broken sentences her terrible fear of having the facts known; her despair over the tissue of falsehood and truth that she had told Mr. Patton; her fear of seeing her lover again until she was sure of herself; her grief for Julie's death and her self-accusation of it; her terror that day when Hortense had told her that I had taken her skirt from my closet. But after a time, she looked up, smiling through her tears.

"I am really only crying over Julie," she said. "The rest is all gone, Miss Adams. I am cured—really cured! Today I sat for an hour with a bottle of cocaine beside me, and I did not touch it!"

That was my first case for Mr. Patton. And, though I really discovered nothing that Clare would not have told eventually herself, he was kind enough to say some very pleasant things.

"Though," he said, wincing as he tried to move his leg, "courage carried to the nth power is often foolishness! What possessed you to go to that house alone?"

"I wanted to locate the Landing of the Pilgrims."

He leaned back and looked up at me, smiling.

"Curiosity!" he said. "That was the only quality I was afraid you lacked." He took an envelope from the stand at his elbow and held it out.

"Your check, as per agreement."

"I don't want money, Mr. Patton. I—don't think I am silly, but I had my reward—if I deserve one, which, of course, I don't—when I saw Mr. Plummer's eyes last night. She went straight into his arms."

"You won't take the check?"

"No, thank you."

"Then I'll bank it for you. We are going to have some interesting cases together, Miss Adams, but I wish you were back here to look after me. There's a spineless creature here who lets me bully her. Do you know—you're a queer woman! Taking as remuneration the sight of a young girl going into her lover's arms!"

"I've taken most of my pleasures and all of my sentiment vicariously for a number of years," I retorted. "And, even if it's the other person's, sentiment one has to have!"

"Yes," said Mr. Patton, looking at me curiously. "Sentiment one has to have!"

The bag is before me as I write. There are two keys—one to the house in Brickyard Road; the other to the garden door at the March home. The lavender envelope is there and its scrawled note from Clare—simply explained, as are all confusing things when one has a key. The envelope had contained the vial of cocaine that Clare took with her on her flight. It had, of course, come from the pharmacy clerk. I never examined the clipping carefully until today. It is curious to locate one's mental blind spot. I had read it many times.

The reverse is an advertisement for the cure of the drug habit.

About the Author

Dubbed the American Agatha Christie, Mary Roberts Rinehart was born in Pittsburgh in 1876. The author of more than three dozen novels, many of them best-sellers, she was also a prolific writer of plays and short stories, and several of her works were adapted for film and television. She died in New York in 1958.

To see our other great titles,
visit us at:

BLACKBIRD BOOKS
www.bbirdbooks.com